# A Giant First-Start Reader

This easy reader contains only 45 different words,
repeated often to help the young reader develop
word recognition and interest in reading.

Basic word list for *Joey the Jack-o'-lantern*

| | | |
|---|---|---|
| a | he | scared |
| after | how | scary |
| all | is | she |
| along | it | spooky |
| and | jack-o'-lantern | the |
| are | Joey | time |
| bat | Kate | to |
| be | Manny | tried |
| Billy | matter | wanted |
| but | monster | was |
| came | no | what |
| cat | not | w-h-o-o-o! |
| for | of | Willie |
| Halloween | poor | witch |
| happy | said | you |

# Joey the Jack-O'-Lantern

Written by Janet Craig

Illustrated by Susan Miller

## Troll Associates

*Library of Congress Cataloging in Publication Data*

Joey the Jack-O'-Lantern.

Summary: Joey the jack-o'-lantern longs to be
scary for Halloween, but no one is frightened until
Willie Witch lends her help to Joey.
[1. Pumpkin—Fiction.  2. Halloween—Fiction]
I. Miller, Susan, 1956-       ill.  II. Title.
PZ7.P1762Jo       1988       [E]       87-10845
ISBN 0-8167-1105-4 (lib. bdg.)
ISBN 0-8167-1106-2 (pbk.)

10    9    8    7    6    5    4

*W-h-o-o-o!*
Joey was a jack-o'-lantern.

He wanted to be spooky.
He wanted to be scary.

Joey wanted to be scary for Halloween.

Was Joey scary? Was Joey spooky?

No, he was not!

No matter how he tried,
Joey was not spooky.

Along came Kate Cat.

Was Kate scared of Joey?

No! No, she was not!

Along came Billy Bat.
Was Billy scared of Joey?

No! No, he was not!

Along came Manny Monster.
Was Manny scared of Joey?

No! No, he was not!

Poor Joey the jack-o'-lantern.
He tried and tried.

But he was not scary.

Along came Willie Witch.

"Joey," she said. "It is Halloween.
It is time for you to be scary."

Along came Kate Cat.

*W-h-o-o-o!*
"You are scary, Joey!"

Along came Billy Bat.

*W-h-o-o-o!*
"What a spooky jack-o'-lantern!"

Along came Manny Monster.

"Joey, you are scary, after all!"

What a Happy Halloween for Joey the jack-o'-lantern!

*W-h-o-o-o!*

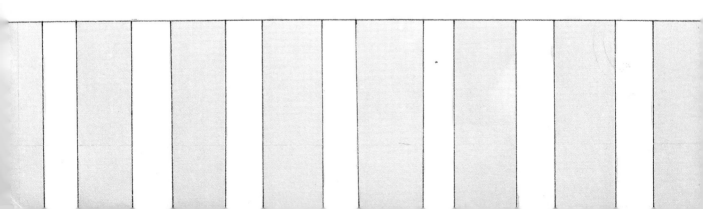